Are we there?

An Ivy and Mack story

Written by Rebecca Colby

Illustrated by Gustavo Mazali

with Nadene Naude

Collins

What's in this story?

Listen and say

castle

helmet

dream

horse

School was finished for the summer holidays.

"Hooray!" said Mack.

"Hooray!" said Ivy.

They were in the car. Ivy saw a motorbike. Mack saw a helicopter.

"We're going somewhere fun!" said Dad.
"Where?" asked Ivy and Mack.
"A great place," said Mum.

Mack's eyes grew big. "Is it a different country?"

Dad laughed. "No, but it is exciting."

Mum showed Ivy and Mack a picture.
"What's this?"

"It's a castle!" said Mack.

Dad stopped the car at the petrol station.

"Are we there?" asked Ivy and Mack.

"No," said Dad. He bought bottles
of lemonade.

They walked by the river.

After their walk by the river, Mack fell asleep.

He had a dream about a castle.

Ivy had a dream about a castle, too.

Mack woke up. "Let's play the *20 Questions Game!*"

"Yes, Dad," said Ivy. "We ask and you answer."

"OK. Mack, you start," said Dad.

"Can we sleep in the castle?" asked Mack.

"Yes!" said Dad.

"Does the castle have horses?" asked Ivy.

"Yes," said Dad.

Ivy had one more question. "Are we there?
I'm tired."

They stopped for a picnic.
"Who's hungry?" asked Mum.

"Look! We're here!" said Mack.

"This is a different castle," said Dad.
"But let's go and look!"

After lunch, Ivy and Mack went into the shop.

There were lots of clothes and toys.

"I need a helmet!" said Mack.

Ivy put on a hat.

In the afternoon, Mum drove the car.

"Let's play *'Name that Song'*," said Mack.

"I love that game," said Dad. He put the tablet down.

"Oh, no!" said Mum. "I drove in a big circle!"

Ivy crossed her arms. "That's the same picnic table!"

"And the same castle!" said Mack.

Mum and Dad found the right road. Ivy and Mack played the *Alphabet Game.*

"I see the letter A—arm," said Mack.

Ivy pointed at Mack's legs. "Well, I see the letter T—trousers."

"Are we there?" they asked.

"No," said Mum and Dad.

Ivy and Mack told funny stories.
They laughed and laughed.

"Let's play the *'Quiet Game'*," said Mum.

All the cars stopped moving. They were in a traffic jam.

"Oh no!" said Mum. "Look at all these cars."

"Are we there?" asked Mack and Ivy.

"It's only ten minutes now," said Dad.

It was evening and the sky was red and purple. The castle was beautiful.

"There it is!" said Ivy.

"Wow!" said Mack.

"We're here!" said Mum and Dad.

The castle had a very big theme park. They went there the next day.

There was a river with boats, and lots of different rides. There were horses and zebras.

"There's so much to do," said Ivy.

"Can we go on *everything*?" asked Mack.

They went on the biggest ride in the park.

"I can see all the people!" said Mack.

"It's fantastic!" said Ivy.

"But, Dad," they said. "Can we not go home today in the car, please?"

Picture dictionary

Listen and repeat

castle　　　helicopter　　　motorbike

petrol station　　　river

theme park　　　traffic jam

1 Look and order the story

2 Listen and say

Collins

Published by Collins
An imprint of HarperCollins*Publishers*
Westerhill Road
Bishopbriggs
Glasgow
G64 2QT

HarperCollins*Publishers*
1st Floor, Watermarque Building
Ringsend Road
Dublin 4
Ireland

William Collins' dream of knowledge for all began with the publication of his first book in 1819.

A self-educated mill worker, he not only enriched millions of lives, but also founded a flourishing publishing house. Today, staying true to this spirit, Collins books are packed with inspiration, innovation and practical expertise. They place you at the centre of a world of possibility and give you exactly what you need to explore it.

© HarperCollins*Publishers* Limited 2020

10 9 8 7 6 5 4 3 2

ISBN 978-0-00-839831-6

Collins® and COBUILD® are registered trademarks of HarperCollins*Publishers* Limited

www.collins.co.uk/elt

British Library Cataloguing in Publication Data

A catalogue record for this publication is available from the British Library.

Author: Rebecca Colby
Lead illustrator: Gustavo Mazali (Beehive)
Copy illustrator: Nadene Naude (Beehive)
Series editor: Rebecca Adlard
Commissioning editor: Zoë Clarke
Publishing manager: Lisa Todd
Product managers: Jennifer Hall and Caroline Green
In-house editor: Alma Puts Keren
Project manager: Emily Hooton
Editor: Deborah Friedland
Proofreaders: Natalie Murray and Michael Lamb
Cover designer: Kevin Robbins
Typesetter: 2Hoots Publishing Services Ltd
Audio produced by id audio, London
Reading guide author: Julie Penn
Production controller: Rachel Weaver
Printed and bound by: GPS Group, Slovenia

Download the audio for this book and a reading guide
for parents and teachers at www.collins.co.uk/839831